Praise for Amelia Elia's *Chosen*

"I have read all three of her stories in this series and loved every one of them... all three are just outstanding reads. Bravo to Amelia Elias for sharing her talent with us [in CHOSEN] and bringing us The Guardians' League!"

~ *Recommended Read from Twolips Reviews*

"Fast-paced, intriguing, and with just enough heat to leave you breathless, CHOSEN is one that shouldn't be missed."

~ *Romance Reviews Today*

"CHOSEN is the sexiest, most fun Guardians' League book yet. I recommend it to everyone, even if you don't ordinarily like vampire stories. CHOSEN and the rest of The Guardians' League books are not to be missed."

~ *5 Hearts from The Romance Studio*

Chosen

Book Three of the Guardians' League

Amelia Elias

A Samhain Publishing, Ltd. publication.

Samhain Publishing, Ltd.
512 Forest Lake Drive
Warner Robins, GA 31093
www.samhainpublishing.com

Chosen
Copyright © 2008 by Amelia Elias
Print ISBN: 1-59998-725-2
Digital ISBN: 1-59998-444-X

Editing by Jessica Bimberg
Cover by Anne Cain

First Samhain Publishing, Ltd. electronic publication: April 2007
First Samhain Publishing, Ltd. print publication: February 2008

Dedication

This book is dedicated with best wishes to my brother Eric and his bride-to-be, Marcella. May you enjoy many happy years together, and may your love grow ever stronger. (Yay, I get to be an aunt!)

And many thanks are due to Jess Bimberg, editor extraordinaire, for flexibility, patience, and support above and beyond the call of duty. Words cannot express my appreciation and thanks, but these two come close—you rock!

Chapter One

"You *can't* just say no."

Alexa raised an eyebrow and gripped her glass until her knuckles ached. "You're right," she said, hoping her face wasn't flaming. The heat pouring from her cheeks didn't reassure her. "I'll rephrase it. *Hell,* no."

From the laughter of her friends, Alexa knew she wasn't getting off that easily. Grace grinned from beneath the condom-bedecked veil the others had forced on her and waved her sword-shaped swizzle stick threateningly, sending the olive sliding to a precarious halt right at the tip. "Don't disobey the bride at a bachelorette party, missy. No one made you pick 'dare'. I love you like a sister, but shut up, get up, and pay up."

Alexa winced. "Come on, Grace," she tried again, sending her most pitiful look toward the woman she'd thought was her friend. "I'm nowhere near drunk enough to do that!"

They all laughed again. "And you won't ever get that drunk, if I know you," Heather said.

"Yeah, girl, you really need to loosen up," Kim joined in. "When's the last time you actually touched a male?"

"And not to take a temp or change a dressing?" Grace added.

"Guys, you'd cry if she told you. It's measured in years," Kim said, shaking her head sadly as her eyes twinkled with mischief.

She glared at all of them. "Traitor," she muttered at Kim. Then she sighed. It was clear she wasn't getting out of this. What devil had possessed her when she'd picked dare? These were the very same girls who'd been trying—unsuccessfully—to get her laid ever since she'd been transferred to the ICU. After six months of getting copies of every single study listing the health benefits of regular sex, every article showing the links between frequent intercourse and reduced depression, cervical cancer, and suicide, and every possible translation of the Kama Sutra, Alexa should've known what to expect. They said they had her best interests at heart, but she'd been unable to persuade any of them that her best interests didn't reside below her waist.

Most people thought nurses were angels of mercy. She knew firsthand they could be absolutely ruthless when the mood took them.

"Fine," she said, putting down her soda and standing up. She glanced around the bar, searching for the most non-threatening man she could find and praying he'd be in the darkest possible corner.

"No, you don't," Grace said as though reading her mind. She scanned the bar for a moment before her eyes lit up and she grinned again. "Oh my God, someone remind me quick that I love John. Check that guy out! Over there, talking to Luc at the bar."

Everyone but Alexa turned and every last one of them looked back at her with matching evil grins. Grace winked at her. "Go say hello to your new friend, Alexa."

Alexa turned to look with a sinking feeling in the pit of her stomach. Her jaw dropped when she caught a glimpse of the man chatting with Grace's bartender friend. Tall, blond, and dressed in leather from head to toe, he was the epitome of everything Alexa had been avoiding for the last two years. He laughed and half-turned, denying her the sight of his impossibly tight butt lovingly cupped in black leather only to gift her with a glimpse of a face that would make Michelangelo's David green with envy.

He reached for his glass and his jacket parted, revealing nothing beneath but golden skin and enough rippling muscle to wipe every coherent thought from her head. On anyone else, such an outfit might've made her question his orientation, but not on this guy. He radiated danger and masculinity, and sweet, hot seduction.

Adonis in black leather. He looked like the kind of bad news every girl secretly dreamed of finding.

Every girl but her, that was. Adonis laughed and Alexa groaned. She couldn't believe Grace was actually making her do this, but further protests would only delay the inevitable. Taking a deep breath for courage, she turned her back on her friends and started across the crowded bar as though walking to her doom, pretending she didn't hear their ribald shouts of "encouragement".

She stopped behind Adonis and took another breath to steady her nerves. She instantly wished she hadn't as his subtle aftershave swept over her—not too much, not too strong, and sexy as hell. Why it surprised her, she couldn't say. Every inch of this guy was pure sex, and at well over six feet tall, that was a lot of sexy inches.

Don't go there, Alexa. Stop that thought right there.

Before she could chicken out—a thought that was all too tempting—she reached out and tapped him on the shoulder. "Excuse me," she said through a throat that felt much too tight. "Can I ask a favor?"

Adonis turned and her heart leapt into her throat. Up close he was even more devastating than he'd been from across the bar. Eyes the color of warm gunmetal met hers as he smiled at her.

"Hello," he said, his deep voice caressing nerves she'd spent the last two years convincing herself she didn't even have. He caught her hand and lifted it to his lips, his mouth skimming her knuckles in a gesture as gallant as it was unexpected. Her heart kicked against her ribs. "For you, anything," he added, not releasing her hand.

For a moment Alexa couldn't even speak. For Adonis to have the voice of a sex god and the manners of a knight was just too, too unfair. The urge to flee almost overtook her and she blurted the words before she could give in and run. "It's a dare. I mean Truth or Dare. I mean... Oh, hell, I have to do a body shot with you."

One golden eyebrow raised and for a second that was all. Then Adonis smiled. Not grinned, *smiled.* Kindly. "Nervous?" he asked as his thumb traced a feather-soft caress over her inner wrist.

That caress tingled all the way up her arm and down her spine before settling low in her belly as a curl of liquid heat. If she hadn't tied her hair back she was sure it would be standing on end.

"You don't have to if you don't want to," she said, her cheeks so hot it felt like she could fry an egg on them. She didn't want to imagine the torture that would follow if he told her no. It was too horrible to contemplate.

He leaned close and murmured in her ear, "I wouldn't miss it for the world, sweetheart, but I want nothing you don't wish to give. Do *you* want to do this, or do you want me to help you get out of it?"

Alexa closed her eyes for just a moment, unable to stop herself from savoring the sensation of his breath on the sensitive skin of her ear and the warmth of his hard body inches from hers. This man was not the arrogant jerk she'd first assumed. He was quickly moving into too-good-to-be-true territory with that offer to rescue her from her pushy friends. There was nothing he could've done that would have surprised her more, and her reaction to it was downright shocking.

"Let's do it."

He chuckled in her ear and she shivered from head to toe. "Words no man can ever resist," he teased before pulling back. He released her hands and spread his arms. "I'm all yours, sweetheart. Do with me what you will."

She laughed. "Has that line actually worked for you?"

He smiled, but his eyes were serious. "More importantly, is it working now?"

Alexa chose to ignore that—she could handle a little light teasing, but serious flirting with Adonis was out of the question. She turned to the bartender to order a tequila shot and found one already waiting for her, a shaker of salt and a lime on a napkin beside it. The bartender, Luc, was leaning against the bar, his eyes twinkling. "Give him hell, girl."

"More like heaven, if you ask me," the guy on the next barstool commented.

Luc laughed and opened his mouth to say something else but Adonis cut him off. "Leave the lady alone," he commanded. There was no other word for it. His voice shimmered with authority though his eyes never left Alexa. "Where do you want me?"

Now that was a loaded question if she'd ever heard one. She cleared her throat and summoned a smile of her own as she lifted the shot, salt, and lime. If she really had to do this, she'd make it something even a man like him would remember.

"On the bar," she said. That golden eyebrow rose again and her grin widened. "On your back."

Luc laughed and the other guy gave a low whistle as the people around them lifted their drinks, but Adonis said nothing. He braced his hands on the bar and lifted himself up with one smooth ripple of muscle before turning and lying back in the vacated space, knees bent. One big boot rested on the bar and the other on his barstool. Alexa could all but feel her friends' disbelief radiating across the crowded bar but refused to turn around and glance at them. The slide of his jacket across that golden skin as he laced his fingers behind his head, silently giving her free run of his body, had her full attention.

And what a body it was. She gave herself a moment to stare, wishing she could take an hour to give this man the attention he was due. His jacket fell completely open, exposing a palm-sized tattoo of a spider on his left side. She touched it with a fingertip, wincing at the thought of needles in such a sensitive area. "That must've hurt."

He winked at her. "Other things have hurt more."

It was a perfect opening and she absolutely wasn't going there. Her fingertip left his side and traced a circle around his navel. "If I put the glass here, will it spill?"

A quiver ran through his muscles and a wave of purely feminine satisfaction made her bite her lip. He watched the movement like a hawk.

"'Fraid so," Adonis said, still gazing at her mouth. "I'm only human."

Luc laughed again and Adonis shot him a glare. Alexa ignored it.

"I guess I'll have to get creative, then." She set the shot aside and lifted the lime and salt. "Ready?"

His eyes smoldered when he answered. "I've been ready all my life, sweetheart."

She lifted the lime to his lips. He opened his mouth willingly, his gaze never leaving her face as she positioned the lime between his teeth. His warm breath tickled her fingers and she could almost believe it had quickened in anticipation. When she had the lime just how she wanted it, she lifted the salt and glanced down his body, her own breath coming a little faster at the thought of where to sprinkle it.

Her attention kept returning to the strong column of his throat. She could see his pulse throbbing temptingly just above the collarbone. As she stared, the throbbing sped up. Before she could talk herself out of it, Alexa bent and ran her tongue over the spot.

His low hiss of pleasure thrilled her. She licked his skin again, closing her eyes to better savor the warmth of his skin beneath her lips, the slight saltiness on her tongue. She couldn't resist one final swirl before she pulled away and sprinkled salt over the spot, not quite daring to look up into his eyes and see if he was as affected as she was.

Ignoring the shot glass by his hip, Alexa dropped the salt shaker onto the bar and returned to his throat. This time he groaned aloud as she painstakingly licked every bit of the salt away, taking her time and making a very thorough job of it. Obeying an instinct she didn't even know she had, she nipped at his skin right over his pulse and was rewarded with what sounded like a low oath muffled by the lime as he shivered. She couldn't resist doing it again. She knew she should stop this before she marked him, but his obvious pleasure at what she was doing made it hard for her to think rationally.

Only then did she lift the shot glass and meet his eyes. The desire in his gaze was enough to send molten heat through her veins. She winked at him before bending to his navel and filling it with tequila. He groaned again in anticipation and Alexa quickly bent and sucked the liquor from his body. A tiny rivulet escaped and she chased it down with her tongue as it rolled down his side. His body arched like a bow when she flicked her tongue into his navel to make sure she'd gotten every last drop.

Finally she made herself pull away and quickly bit the lime, keeping her eyes closed so she didn't have to look at his expression. His breath definitely came faster, just like hers. He angled his head to give her greater access as she sucked the tart juice from the fruit. His lips were firm and warm against hers and Alexa pulled back from that temptation almost at once. She was already far too close to getting seriously carried away here.

When she pulled away she realized half the bar was cheering and knew she should be mortified, but when Adonis swung his legs off the bar and caught her in his arms, everything else faded to the background. She saw his intention in his burning eyes a moment before his mouth descended and got her fingers between them just in time. "Not on a first date, Adonis," she murmured, his lips kept from hers by nothing more than the width of her finger.

"Gareth," he corrected, still holding her against his bare chest and making no move to pull away. His lips moving against her finger sent shivers through her entire body. "Gareth Ambrocio."

"Pleased to meet you, Gareth," Alexa said, taking an experimental step back to see if he would try to hold her. He didn't, and she didn't know if she was relieved or disappointed. "Thanks for the favor."

He caught her hand as she pulled it away from those too-tempting lips. "Tell me your name," he said. Demanded. "I need it."

Alexa shook her head, taking another step back. This guy was light-years out of her league. There was no reason to even hope he'd call her even if she did give her name and number, so why leave herself open for the disappointment?

"Goodnight, Gareth," she murmured, then pulled her hand from his and fled.

"Holy Creator, Gareth, I can't believe you just let her walk away!"

"Shut up, Sin."

"No, for once I have to agree with Sin," Luc put in from across the bar. "You've lost it, Gar."

"You can shut up, too."

Sin started to say something else but Gareth wasn't listening. He was staring after the woman who'd just shown up from nowhere and set him afire. She slipped through the crowd effortlessly, all long legs and sexiness hidden beneath plain-Jane jeans and a button-down shirt. Her dark ponytail, so incongruous after the passion she'd just showed, swayed with every step she took. His hands burned to dive into that rich softness as he claimed the kiss he literally ached for.

Maybe Sin and Luc were right. He must've been crazy to let her walk away that easily. Sweet heaven, right now he'd give just about anything he owned to take back that moment when he'd let her stop him from kissing her. The thought of those soft lips against his again was enough to heat his already boiling body another few degrees.

"...know the whole Ambassador gig involves improving vampire-human relations, but damn, I didn't realize it meant *that* kind of relations!"

Luc laughed at Sin and Gareth rolled his eyes. The Cobra Clan Patriarch was only five hundred or so, a mere babe compared to Gareth, and at times Sin seemed as immature as a teenager. It was a good thing Gareth's own twelve centuries had taught him patience. Otherwise the continual stream of wisecracks would have really pissed him off.

As it was, they were only damn annoying.

Sin finished off his wine—a rich merlot whose deep burgundy hue disguised the fact that it was mixed with something much richer—and set his glass back down with a decisive *thunk*, his eyes still on the dark-haired woman. He slapped Gareth on the shoulder and started to stand.

"Your wine is excellent, Luc, but I've got a hunger for a different vintage. If you'll excuse me," he said with a grin, "I think I've just got to have a taste of that."

Luc frowned—he allowed no hunting in his bar, Clan Patriarch or not—but Gareth's attention snapped fully back to the present and he spoke before Luc could so much as take a breath.

"First Right," Gareth said, the words out almost before he knew what he was saying.

Sin froze in the middle of rising from his barstool. It took him a moment to find his voice. "I know I heard that wrong."

"Think, Gar," Luc murmured, and Gareth didn't need to glance at him to know the bartender was staring at him like he'd grown a second head.

He didn't care. It was too late to take it back, and even so Gareth wasn't certain he would have. His mystery woman was a lucky find indeed. He couldn't believe the others hadn't sensed it, but then again, neither of them had been born dhampyr as he had.

"First Right," he repeated in a low growl. "I claim her. Don't even think about it, Sin."

If Sin was serious in his own pursuit, he could make a challenge of his own right now. Luc watched them both warily as tension vibrated in the air between them. Sin's Clan was large and strong—the Cobras were not to be taken lightly—and every one of them would fight if their Patriarch required it.

But Gareth's Clan was almost equal in size, and Gareth's own personal power couldn't be discounted.

Sin sat back down without issuing a challenge, however, and finally managed to close his mouth with an audible snap. "You ever hear of the term *overreaction*, Gareth?" he asked, a ghost of his teasing grin returning as he tried to ease things back to a calmer tone. "If you didn't want me to sample your human all you had to do was ask, not claim courtship rights."

Gareth's muscles relaxed minutely. "Luc's bar is off-limits for hunting," he replied, his tone so low that no mortals could overhear him.

"This was to stop me from breaking Luc's house rules?" He shook his head and laughed. "Again I say, overreaction, but I wish you luck and the Creator's blessing. Now, if we've concluded our business here, might I suggest finding a snack elsewhere?"

"You go ahead," Gareth declined. He needed to feed but there was no way he was leaving the bar just yet. He could just glimpse the brunette across the bar as she shook her head apologetically at a man who'd clearly just asked her to dance. "I have a little unfinished business here. The hospitality of my House is at your disposal after you see to your needs."

Sin inclined his head and smiled. "I leave you to your own hunt, then," he said. With a nod in Luc's direction, he turned and left.

Luc refilled Gareth's glass without being asked. "Are you really going to court her?" he asked as he retrieved Sin's abandoned goblet. "You didn't have to do that just to keep him from breaking my rules, you know. I could have taken care of it."

"I didn't," Gareth said, and he meant it. That woman was special, a rare breed indeed, and he'd known it at the first sound of her voice. He blessed his own mixed heritage for alerting him to it before Sin or Luc noticed that the brunette who had so utterly rocked his world was a dhampyr.

The half-vampires were rare and highly prized. Their blood was intoxicating, their powers were unique, and the females were the only vampires capable of conceiving. If Sin had recognized her for what she was, Gareth was certain a challenge would have been issued. Wars were fought for less. For an unmated Patriarch without an heir, finding a dhampyr was too good of an opportunity to miss.

The fact that she was gorgeous and had a mouth that could set him ablaze was just an added bonus.

He tossed off his glass of bloodwine in one go and stood. He might have claimed the right to be the first to court her, but she wasn't his until he won her. Once the others figured out her heritage, he'd have plenty of competition. He didn't dare waste any time.

"Play a slow song for me, will you?" he said as he turned toward her table and pretended not to see Luc roll his eyes.

The crowd was thick and it took him a few minutes to make his way to the woman's table. His gaze caressed her back as he approached, admiring the fine line of her slender shoulders and straight spine. One by one her friends noticed him and fell silent. He smiled and paused behind the brunette's chair.

"Excuse me," he said, and he saw her jump. "I wondered if I might have this dance."

She turned in her chair and froze when she saw him. Her cocoa eyes widened, looking for all the world like a deer caught in headlights. "I—I don't think—no," she stammered.

"What?" one of her friends gasped.

"Yes, she wants to dance," the woman in the hideous veil said sternly. "Alexa, get up right this second and dance with the man!"

Alexa. At last he had a name for her. Gareth smiled at the bride-to-be before meeting Alexa's gaze again. "No," he said, holding up a hand as she started to rise with clear reluctance.

She was skittish, distrustful, and he knew he wouldn't accomplish anything by pressuring her. "Nothing you don't wish to give," he murmured, stepping back. "Remember?"

Alexa stared at him, stunned as he turned and walked away. She'd sent away two other men tonight and neither had taken it nearly this well, and to be brutally honest, neither of them could hold a candle to Gareth. It was unbelievable that he'd followed her to the table in the first place and even more so that he'd backed off so easily.

"What the hell were you thinking?" Kim demanded, gaping at her. "The man is a walking god and he was looking at you like he'd like to cover you in chocolate and lick you clean. Are you stupid, girl? Have you taken a vow of celibacy or something?"

That got her temper going and she embraced the welcome distraction. "Look, people, just because all of you happen to be in relationships and happily boinking away every night doesn't mean you get to pick on me because I'm not!" Alexa pushed her chair back and stood. "I'm getting more than a little tired of all of you trying to push everything in pants my way. I've already done your stupid little dare and that's enough for one night. Now drop it!"

There was a moment of stunned silence before Grace also stood. "All right, Alexa," she said. "All right. We'll lay off. We didn't mean to push so hard, did we, girls?" There was a chorus of agreement. "It's just that you seem so lonely sometimes, we just wanted to help."

"I don't need any help," Alexa said, starting to feel embarrassed about her outburst. After all, this was Grace's party. The bride-to-be should be enjoying center stage, not Alexa. "Let's just forget the whole thing, okay? Next round's on me."

She waved to their server and tried not to notice Gareth chatting with a stunning blonde on the dance floor, but it was like asking a magnet not to attract iron. Good Lord, the man was hot! Her gaze was drawn back to him time and again as the evening wore on. Every time he laughed, she could've sworn she felt it down her spine. Every time he danced with another woman, she couldn't repress the regret that it wasn't her. Every time he started to glance her way, she pretended to be blithely having the time of her life, totally unaware of him.

She wondered if she was really fooling him. Somehow, she didn't think so.

She couldn't even explain to herself why she'd refused to dance with him. Something about him was very disconcerting...disconcerting and yet familiar. The way he walked, the glint of humor in those gunmetal eyes, the tilt of his blond head as he glanced her way from the corner of his eye—it was like déjà vu to the power of ten.

When Kim yawned two hours later, Alexa could've wept with relief. After her little tantrum she hadn't wanted to be the first to leave, but she'd been ready to go home an hour ago. The little party broke up at last with hugs and laughter, and ribald teasing when they refused to let Grace take off her veil to walk to her car.

"Come on, guys, this isn't Mardi Gras!" she complained.

"Honey, it's still Bourbon Street," Heather told her. "Anything goes, and it took us hours to figure out how to hot-glue those things on there. Do you have any idea how hard it is to get latex to stick to netting?"

They reached the car a few minutes later and Heather, Kim and Grace climbed in. "Sure you don't want a ride?" Heather asked. "It's pretty late. You should've brought your ride."

"It wasn't worth trying to start the Vespa for just a couple of blocks," Alexa said, shaking her head. "And the Quarter is pretty heavily patrolled on the weekends. I'll be fine."

When the car pulled away, Alexa turned and started walking toward her apartment. Despite the expense, she loved her little flat overlooking Bourbon Street. It was tiny, but it was hers and it was home. Besides, it had a great view of the floats during Mardi Gras and there was room in the garden to park her little Vespa.

The night was cool and humid. Alexa breathed deep and let it out slowly, savoring the evening air. She loved the nights, when the fumes from cars and tour buses were at their lowest and the stars winked down at her as if trying to share secrets.

"Bit late for an evening stroll, isn't it?"

She gasped and spun, her hand diving into her purse for her pepper spray even as the shiver coursing down her spine identified the speaker. "Are you following me?" she demanded as Gareth stepped into view.

He shrugged. "It's not safe for a woman to walk the streets alone at this hour," he said, not denying her accusation. "Why didn't you let your friends give you a ride?"

He stepped closer and Alexa backed up. He stopped at once and held up his hands. "I won't hurt you," he said softly. "I just want to see you home safe, nothing more. All right?"

The sixth sense she tried to pretend she didn't have told her he spoke the truth. He wasn't following her for some nefarious purpose. Still, she didn't make a habit of letting strange men know where she lived.

"It's just a few blocks," she said. "I'll be fine. I have my pepper spray and my cell phone if I run into any trouble, so you don't have to worry about me. Okay?"

He shook his head. "I'll worry anyway." That smile flashed again, at once sexy and a bit predatory. "We could stand here arguing about it until the dawn or you could just give in and let me walk you home. I'm very stubborn."

Alexa drew in a breath to refuse but let it out on a sigh. He wasn't lying about that, either. "Oh, all right," she said, giving in. "You can walk with me for a little way, but you have to go away when I tell you to. All right?"

He stepped fully out of the shadows and offered his arm. "Lead the way, my lady," he said with another heart-stopping smile.

It didn't occur to her until later that he never agreed to her condition.

Chapter Two

Alexa swatted the buzzing alarm clock, wishing it was a fly so she could kill it. Why did the snooze button seem to dodge her efforts to hit it?

Finally she made contact and the insufferable noise stopped. She flopped back onto her pillow and pulled the covers over her head. Why, exactly, had she agreed to switch to the night shift? Sleeping all day and working all night just wasn't natural, as her body reminded her every evening when it was time to get up. Even now she had the start of another migraine tensing up behind her eyes, and she'd never had so much as the tiniest headache until a month ago.

The alarm buzzed again and Alexa flung her pillow at it. It tumbled to the floor but didn't stop its noise. She sighed and swung her legs out of bed before smacking the "off" switch with far more force than necessary.

Served the damn thing right for making that horrible sound, anyway.

Thirty minutes and two cups of coffee later, she felt much closer to human. Alexa tucked her long braid down the collar of her jacket, slid her helmet and gloves on, and went down to the garden. Her little blue Vespa started on the first try—definitely a plus these days—and moments later, she was driving down the cobbled streets.

The fresh air cleared the last of the sleep from her mind, but it didn't stay fresh for long. She got caught first behind a bus and then behind a dump truck, and traffic was too heavy for her to pass for several minutes. At last she reached the hospital and pulled into the parking garage with relief.

Her arrival on the floor normally didn't attract attention, even if she was a few minutes late this time, but not tonight. As soon as she stepped out of the elevator and into the ICU, Heather squealed her name.

"Ooh, she's here! Finally, girl! We've been dying of curiosity. Come tell us who they're from!"

Alexa frowned blankly at her. "Who are what from?"

"Oh, you're just going to die. Come on, come look!"

Heather grabbed her arm and dragged her into the tiny combination break room/locker room. There in the center of the rickety old table was the most exquisite bouquet of flowers she'd ever seen. Alexa gaped at them. There had to be two dozen roses in there, not to mention exotic lilies, orchids, and flowers for which she had no name.

"You've got to be joking," she whispered, dropping her helmet on one of the chairs and circling the enormous floral arrangement. "There's no way those are for me. Someone made a mistake."

"No, your name is on the card," Heather said, pointing.

Alexa reached for the little card with a feeling of complete disbelief. "Alexa," it said in a bold cursive scrawl. She closed her eyes, suddenly knowing where they'd come from. There was only one person in the world who'd shown any sort of interest in her in the last two years.

Even the masculine, self-assured handwriting practically screamed Gareth.

"Aren't you going to open it?"

Heather was practically bouncing with excitement. Alexa sighed and tore open the card. "My lady," it said, "a small token of thanks for the midnight stroll." It wasn't signed.

Darn him, he was so confident he could send a hundred dollar bouquet and not even sign his name to the card?

"Omigosh! It's him, isn't it? It's the guy from the club!"

She'd forgotten Heather was standing there, reading over her shoulder. "I think it is," she admitted. "He walked me home after you guys left."

"How romantic," Heather gushed. "Alexa, if you don't snatch this guy up then I will. Can you believe he went to all this trouble?"

Alexa slid the card back into its envelope and stuffed it in her pocket. "The guy's probably a stalker," she said, turning her back on the flowers. "How did he know where I work? I certainly never told him. And we'd better be extra careful to keep this door closed until I can get these things out of here." No flowers or plants were allowed near the fragile ICU patients. "I can't believe y'all even accepted the delivery! What if someone's allergic to pollen?"

Heather rolled her eyes. "Here you have a gorgeous guy sending you gorgeous flowers and all you can think of is pollen. You're hopeless, girl." She turned and pulled open the door. "Come on, it's time for report."

Alexa slipped into a seat and took notes as the evening nurses reported on the patients and their conditions, but her mind kept returning to those flowers. How *had* he found out where she worked, anyway? She chewed on the end of her pen, trying to keep her mind on her work. She'd been so certain he was telling the truth when he'd promised he wouldn't hurt her. Had she been wrong to let him walk her home?

When report was finally over, Alexa followed the other nurses out. She grabbed her clipboard and went in to check on her patients for the evening—an elderly man recovering from a major heart attack, who slept through her check, and a young woman with complications from a C-section. A photograph of her tiny newborn was taped to her bedrail and she traced the wrinkled little face with a fingertip.

"How are you feeling tonight?" Alexa asked, smiling as she entered the small, glass-walled room. "Any better?"

A tear slipped down the woman's cheek. "I just want to hold him," she whispered. "Just for a minute. Why can't I hold him?"

The woman's pain was sharp and piercing. Alexa took a slow breath as it washed through her, released the air and let the pain slip away. "You've got a pretty bad infection, Mrs. Fielding," she explained gently. "I know you don't want to expose your son to that."

"It's Lily," the woman said, her hand trembling and finally dropping down from the picture. Her weakness alarmed Alexa. Lily hadn't been this bad when she'd cared for her two nights ago. "What if I die without ever holding my baby?"

Alexa put down the clipboard and took the woman's hand. "You won't die," she said softly. She knew that anyone who overheard her would think she was breaking the age-old rule of the medical profession—never promise what can't be guaranteed. Lily's condition wasn't good. She'd bled badly during the C-section, the infection in her womb had spread to her blood, and she had a blood clot in her leg from her forced immobility. She was allergic to the most effective antibiotic for her infection. Everything that could go wrong seemed to be doing so. The physicians gave her a fifty-fifty shot at pulling through even with all the state-of-the-art medical treatment she was receiving. No one could promise a full recovery.

But Alexa could at least promise life.

"You won't die," she repeated, stroking Lily's hair back from her face and smiling down at her. "Rest now. I'll be back in a little while to check up on you, and we'll talk a little more before my shift ends. All right?"

Lily dried her eyes with the corner of the sheet and nodded.

"All right. Rest and dream of your little boy. You'll see him soon."

Back at the desk, Alexa concentrated on her charting. It was a quiet night in the ICU, a rare occurrence but a welcome one. They had one new admission from the ER, one patient who couldn't sleep, and nothing else. The nurses chatted quietly, mindful of the patients sleeping fitfully just feet away, and watched the monitors for any changes. Every so often a nurse would slip away to administer a medication or take vital signs. It was as close to peaceful as the ICU ever was.

For Alexa, it was a mixed blessing. She pulled down Lily's chart and pretended to read it as she steeled herself for what was to come. It had been a long time since she'd attempted this with someone so very ill. The quiet gave her time to collect her thoughts, but it also meant that the other nurses were more likely to catch her when she returned to Lily's cubicle. She just wished her head would stop pounding before she tried it.

There was no help for it. An hour before her shift was to end, Alexa took her stethoscope and blood pressure cuff into Lily's enclosure. The woman was sleeping deeply thanks to the morphine drip the doctor had ordered for the pain. That, too, would help. It was much harder for Alexa to do this if they were awake and watching her with questions in their eyes.

She pulled the bedside chair closer and wrapped the cuff around Lily's arm but did not inflate it. Instead, she covered both of the woman's fever-hot hands with her own and closed her own eyes. She matched her breathing to Lily's and, when the rhythm of her lungs and heart was just right, merged with her.

The infection was a living thing, vicious and tenacious. It was everywhere. Alexa didn't panic or hesitate. She envisioned searing heat attacking every microbe, an army of tiny fireballs hunting them down throughout the young mother's body. Careful not to raise her body temperature too high, she worked slowly, following the heat with waves of soothing cool to envelop and soothe every damaged organ. It was a delicate balance. Too much heat and Lily's fever would rage out of control and result in brain damage or death, but too much of a reprieve between attacks would give the infection time to renew its hold on her body.

The blood clot was a different kind of challenge. She could break it easily but she had to do so carefully. She didn't want to dislodge it as she worked and send it rushing through the woman's veins, a fatal bomb just searching for a place to explode. She chipped slowly away at the exposed edges during the cool reprieves from her battle with the infection, loosening it a cell at a time without disturbing the portion caught on the vessel wall. Finally it dissolved completely.

At last Alexa drove the last particles of infection out and withdrew back into her own body, breathless and shaking. The incision on Lily's belly would leave a scar but Alexa was far too tired to deal with that now. It would heal, that was the important thing.

"You'll hold that baby boy soon, Lily," she whispered, releasing the woman's hands and removing the blood pressure cuff.

"Alexa? You okay?"

She turned and smiled at Heather's voice. "Fine," she replied softly. "I was just praying with her a little, but I think she fell asleep." It was an excuse that had always worked in the past.

"You're a sweetheart," Heather said, smiling. "There's a fresh pot of coffee ready and you look like you could use some."

Alexa managed to make it to the break room without stumbling from exhaustion, but it was a struggle. Her headache was back with a vengeance. The coffee revived her a little and she sat for a moment, eyes closed, the mingled aromas of coffee and flowers filling her senses. She finished her shift on autopilot, too sick from fatigue and pain to do much else. Still, when the morning shift came on and the doctors made their rounds, their astonishment at seeing Lily sitting up in bed, her color back and her eyes bright, brought a smile to Alexa's lips.

Maybe it wasn't nursing as she'd been taught to do it in school, but the look on Lily's face when the doctor told her she could be moved down to a regular unit—a unit that allowed children to visit—made everything worthwhile.

When she gathered up her helmet and gloves at the end of the shift, Alexa couldn't help but glance at the flowers again. She really had to get them out of here, but how was she supposed to transport twenty pounds of flowers on the back of a Vespa? The scent of diesel exhaust on her gloves made her sigh. There was just no way to get them home without ruining them in the process.

It was a real shame. Whatever she might think of the sender, the flowers were absolutely gorgeous and she'd never received anything like them before.

And she wasn't sure just what she thought of the sender. Why was a man like Gareth Ambrocio so interested in her?

Heather interrupted her train of thought by bursting into the room, grinning and waving a roll of cling-film. "You wouldn't believe the begging I had to do to get this from the cafeteria," she said, stepping around Alexa to the flowers. "You'd think this stuff was solid gold, the way they hoard it." Her last words were punctuated with another wave of the film before she started unrolling it.

"May I ask what you're up to?"

"Helping you get your flowers home, of course," she said as though it was completely obvious. "Here, help me wrap them up."

Bemused, Alexa did as she was asked. Minutes later the flowers were encased in cellophane. "All right, I can see how this will keep them from being shredded by the wind, but there's still another problem. Any bright ideas on how to strap this onto my scooter, oh wise one?"

Heather beamed and held up an Ace wrap and a roll of tape. "Come on, let's go exercise those bandaging skills."

Alexa laughed. There was nothing like a nurse's ingenuity. She pulled on her jacket and lifted the flowers, and Heather followed with her helmet and the supplies. It took some doing, but eventually they secured the huge arrangement to the tiny rack behind the Vespa's seat. It looked hideous but it would work. "Thanks, Heather," she said, hugging her friend. "I'll see you tomorrow night."

"Wouldn't miss it."

The drive home, in morning traffic when she was already exhausted, was no picnic. When Alexa finally arrived back in her garden, she was so tired it was all she could do to get herself and the flowers up the stairs. Her head was pounding in earnest now, bright flashes of pain that made every movement agony.

It seemed too much trouble to unwrap the flowers so she just cut the cellophane, tape and elastic bandage off, deciding to risk damaging a few petals in the cause of expediency. The arrangement was a little worse for the wear but still beautiful. She refilled it with water and dragged herself to bed, not even